DRAGON REBEL

Laura Shenton

DRAGON REBEL

Laura Shenton

Iridescent Toad Publishing

Iridescent Toad Publishing.

Cover by Janina Cover Designs.

First edition. ISBN 978-1-913779-20-7

Chapter One

The fluorescent lights buzzed incessantly overhead, bathing the department store in a harsh, artificial glow that seemed designed to make everything look worse than it actually was. The endless rows of mass-produced, garishly coloured clothing appeared even cheaper under the unforgiving illumination, their synthetic fabrics gleaming with an almost offensive shine. Kimberley pressed her fingertips against her temples, trying to massage away the dull throb of a headache that had been threatening to overtake her for the past hour. The end of her shift couldn't come soon enough. Saturdays were always pure chaos in retail, but this particular one felt like it had been specifically cursed by some malevolent deity with a grudge against customer service workers.

Packs of teenagers roamed the aisles like feral creatures hunting for prey, their voices echoing through the store in sharp bursts of banter and laughter. They left destruction in their wake – trails of rumpled shirts pulled halfway off hangers, stacks of jeans with sizes mixed beyond recognition, and piles of discarded accessories scattered across every available surface. The mess spread like a virus, multiplying faster than any single employee could hope to contain it. Outfits that had been carefully curated for display now hung precariously from their racks, while others had given up entirely and pooled in messy heaps on the floor, gathering dust and footprints.

The checkout line had evolved into something almost mythological in its enormity, snaking back towards the entrance in a serpentine path that seemed to grow longer with each passing minute. It had become a constant source of tension, a powder keg of customer frustration just waiting for the smallest spark to explode. The air was thick with the sound of impatient sighs and muttered complaints, punctuated by the occasional sharp comment about the wait time or staffing levels. Kimberley had already been forced to step in twice today to mediate heated arguments over return policies. She had made a solemn resolution to keep her magic out of such mundane disputes. A simple flick of her wrist and a few quietly muttered words might have diffused the situations more efficiently, but using her magic – even the simple, unimpressive spells at her disposal – wasn't worth the risk of drawing unwanted attention to her identity as a witch. Years of experience had taught her the hard way that keeping that particular aspect of herself under wraps was always the wisest course of action.

From her position behind the counter, Kimberley maintained a steady rhythm of scanning receipts with practiced efficiency, her movements automatic after countless hours of repetition. She did her best to tune out the whispered conversation of her co-workers, who had gathered in a tight cluster near the gift-wrap station. They were engaged in their favourite pastime – gossiping about the new assistant manager, a remarkably unremarkable man whose primary talent appeared to be his ability to completely vanish whenever the store descended into its peak periods of chaos. Unlike him,

Kimberley didn't have the luxury of disappearing when things got difficult. At twenty-three, with three solid years of experience under her belt and a hard-earned reputation for being unflappable in the face of retail madness, she had become the de facto leader on the sales floor. Everything inevitably fell to her when things went wrong – and in her experience, things always went wrong in retail, usually in the most spectacular and inconvenient ways possible.

The crackle of static from her radio cut through her thoughts like a knife, the harsh sound making her wince as it aggravated her growing headache.

"Uh, Kimberley?" The hesitant voice belonged to Alice, one of their newest hires who still hadn't quite found her footing in the turbulence of retail life. Her tone carried that particular mix of uncertainty and dread that Kimberley had come to associate with situations that were about to make her day significantly more complicated. "Can you come to the fitting rooms? There's... well, there's a bit of a situation. Actually, maybe more than a bit."

Kimberley released a long, measured sigh, shoving the stack of receipts into a drawer with perhaps more force than strictly necessary before unclipping the radio from her hip. "On my way," she replied briskly, already mentally preparing herself for whatever fresh disaster awaited her attention.

She made her way through the store with purposeful strides, her black ankle boots clicking against the glossy tiles in a steady rhythm that seemed to part the sea of shoppers before her. Her long pink hair, carefully wrangled into a loose braid that morning, swayed with each determined step like a pendulum keeping time with her movement. Kimberley's style had always been as bold as her personality – dark, perfectly tailored jeans that hugged her curves, a snug black top that managed to look both professional and slightly rebellious, and a delicate silver necklace shaped like a crescent moon that caught the light with every step. She looked more like she belonged on the cover of a contemporary noir movie poster than managing the endless tedium of fast fashion retail. Her magic simmered quietly beneath her skin, unremarkable but ever-present, like a low-grade fever she'd learned to live with. She rarely needed it in her day-to-day life, but there were definitely times she wished she could just wave her hand and make all of the store's messes disappear in a shower of sparks.

The fitting rooms were tucked away in a quieter corner of the store, hidden behind heavy velvet curtains that had seen better days but still managed to maintain an air of faded elegance. A line of increasingly irritated customers loitered nearby, clutching armfuls of clothes and shooting daggers with their eyes as Kimberley pushed past them with muttered apologies and promises to handle whatever was causing the delay.

"Excuse me," she repeated like a mantra, brushing aside their complaints with the practiced ease of someone who had long since learned that retail customers' grievances were as endless as they were predictable.

The atmosphere inside the fitting area was so thick with tension it felt like walking into a wall. Alice stood near one of the cubicles, her already pale face now practically colourless with anxiety. She was a willowy girl with wire-rimmed glasses that seemed slightly too big for her face, giving her a perpetually startled expression, and she clutched a clipboard to her chest as though it might shield her from whatever turbulence was unfolding. Beside her stood a woman who looked like she'd quite literally clawed her way out of a punk band's tour van after a particularly rough night. The woman's dark hair was shaved close on one side, the remaining length hanging in jagged spikes that had been dyed a shade of crimson. She wore a battered leather jacket covered in patches and safety pins over a studded tank top that had probably been black at some point, paired with combat boots that looked like they'd survived several wars.

But it wasn't the punk woman who immediately captured and held Kimberley's attention – it was the creature sitting at her feet.

A dragon.

Not one of the towering nightmares from fairy tales and fantasy novels, but a small, sleek creature about the size of a terrier. Its amethyst-coloured scales shimmered under the harsh fluorescent lighting, reflecting little flashes of colour with every nervous shift of its body, like an oil slick made of jewels. Its delicate wings were tucked tightly against its sides in a defensive posture, and its narrow, intelligent eyes darted around the room with an awareness that seemed far too keen for a mere animal.

"She's threatening to leave it here," Alice whispered, her voice tight with barely contained panic as the clipboard in her hands trembled slightly.

Kimberley blinked several times, half-expecting the dragon to disappear like a stress-induced hallucination. "What?!"

The punk woman ran a hand through her hair in a gesture of frustration, her numerous bracelets jangling like wind chimes stripped of their tranquillity. Her scuffed boots shifted slightly against the floor, the faint squeak adding to the tense atmosphere. Her expression was an artful mixture of exasperation and disdain, and her smudged eyeliner only served to make her scowl more pronounced, like a cartoon character's expression of anger made flesh.

"You heard her," the woman snapped, her voice rough and raspy, as though she'd spent years shouting over amplifiers at underground concerts. "This stupid thing's been nothing but trouble since day one. Won't stop getting under my damn feet, keeps setting things on fire when it sneezes, and I've absolutely had it up to here."

The dragon flinched visibly at her tone, lowering its head and curling in on itself in a way that made Kimberley's heart twist despite her better judgment. The creature's distress was painfully obvious, and its body language was so expressive it was almost human.

Kimberley crossed her arms over her chest, her expression hardening into the stern mask she reserved for particularly difficult customers. "You can't just dump a dragon here like it's an unwanted pair of jeans. This isn't an animal shelter."

The woman sneered, stepping closer until Kimberley could smell the stale whiskey and cigarette smoke clinging to her clothes. "What are you, the dragon whisperer? You work in retail, not animal control. Your name tag doesn't exactly scream "magical creature expert".'

"I'm the supervisor on duty," Kimberley shot back, keeping her voice calm but allowing an edge of steel to creep into her tone. "You can't abandon a living creature in a department store."

"Keep the damn thing! See if I care!" The woman spun on her heel with theatrical flair, storming out of the fitting room area with enough force to make the heavy curtains sway violently in her wake. The sound of her boots and the angry jingle of her jewellery faded gradually, leaving behind a thick silence broken only by the distant murmur of customers.

The dragon let out a soft, mournful chirp that sounded almost like a question, drawing Kimberley's attention back to it. It lifted its head cautiously, its amethyst eyes meeting hers with a gaze so piercing and intelligent it seemed impossible that it was anything less than fully sentient. There was something in those eyes that spoke of understanding far beyond what any normal animal should possess.

"Well," Kimberley muttered, crouching down to inspect it more closely. Her headache pulsed in time with her heartbeat. "Looks like you're my problem now. Because clearly what this day needed was an abandoned magical creature crisis."

The dragon tilted its head at a curious angle, regarding her for a long moment before carefully nudging its warm snout against her knee. The touch was tentative, almost hesitant, as though it was testing her reaction or seeking reassurance. Its scales were smooth and warm against her skin, radiating a gentle heat that felt oddly comforting.

"Great," Kimberley said with a sigh, straightening up and brushing off her jeans. "Alice, help me get it to the back office. We'll figure out what to do with it there, preferably before it decides to test out those fire-sneezing capabilities that woman mentioned."

Alice hesitated visibly, clutching her clipboard even tighter until her knuckles went white. "Are you sure that's a good idea? What if it, like... sets the office on fire? Or eats the inventory reports? Or attracts other magical creatures? My training definitely didn't cover dragon management."

Kimberley glanced at the dragon again, studying its body language more carefully. It didn't look dangerous – just scared, confused, and utterly lost, much like many of the new employees on their first day. "It'll be fine. Let's just keep it away from the customers before someone decides to post about it on social media and we end up trending for all the wrong reasons."

Reluctantly, Alice stepped forward, and together they managed to coax the dragon into following them through the store. Kimberley led the way, her mind racing with questions and contingencies, trying to figure out exactly how to deal with an abandoned dragon.

Today had officially crossed the line from merely frustrating to absolutely bizarre. And something in her gut told her that this was only the beginning – that her Saturday was about to get a whole lot weirder. As if retail work wasn't already baffling enough without adding magical creatures to the mix!

Chapter Two

Kimberley shut the door to the back office with a firm click that seemed to echo in the cramped space, her shoulders immediately slumping as she finally allowed herself to exhale properly for what felt like the first time in hours. The room was a claustrophobic monument to retail: a hodgepodge of filing cabinets that had seen better decades, overstuffed shelves threatening to spill their contents at any moment, and a desk so littered with paperwork, empty coffee cups, and mysterious debris that its surface was more theoretical than actual. What might have been someone's forgotten lunch from the previous week sat in one corner, the paper bag radiating an aura of neglect that everyone had wordlessly agreed to ignore. The fluorescent light overhead flickered faintly at irregular intervals, casting an exhausted, sickly glow over the accumulated disarray of countless busy days.

The dragon padded around with surprising grace, its delicate claws clicking against the tile floor in a rhythm that reminded Kimberley of rain on a window. It moved with careful precision, its slender body weaving expertly through the narrow gaps between furniture like water finding its path downhill. Every few steps, it would pause to investigate something new – a dusty corner that probably hadn't seen a vacuum in months, a crumpled receipt bearing the faded marks of countless price adjustments, a stray pencil worn down to a stub. Its amethyst eyes were wide with an almost childlike curiosity that made it hard to remember it was potentially dangerous.

Alice hovered anxiously, her hands maintaining their death grip on the clipboard that seemed less like an office supply and more like a security blanket at this point. "So... what now?" she asked, her voice barely rising above a whisper, as though she feared speaking any louder might provoke the dragon into some catastrophic action.

Kimberley glanced at their unexpected guest, which had discovered a piece of printer paper on the floor and was now nibbling on its edge with surprising delicacy, like a connoisseur sampling a fine dish. "First, we need to calm down and think this through rationally. Second, we figure out how to deal with this little guy without causing a store-wide panic or ending up on the evening news."

The dragon froze mid-nibble at the sound of her voice, its head snapping up with the guilty suddenness of a youngster caught raiding the cookie jar after bedtime. The paper dangled comically from its mouth, one corner torn and soggy with dragon saliva. It blinked at Kimberley with an expression that somehow managed to combine absolute defiance with pure innocence, as if challenging her to scold it while simultaneously claiming complete ignorance of any wrongdoing.

"Hey, cut that out," Kimberley said, making a shooing gesture towards the paper. "That could be important paperwork, and I really don't want to explain to head office why our monthly reports have dragon teeth marks."

The dragon maintained eye contact for a long moment, then deliberately dropped the paper with a soft, musical trill that sounded suspiciously like an apology wrapped in sass. The mangled document fluttered to the floor, joining its brethren in the general mess of the office.

Alice let out a nervous giggle that seemed to surprise even her. "It's... kind of cute, isn't it? Like a scaly puppy with wings. A very dangerous, possibly fire-breathing puppy."

Kimberley arched an eyebrow at her junior colleague. "Sure, it's adorable if you ignore the part where it might accidentally set the store on fire. Or decide to use a wall as a scratching post. Or bite someone who gets too close. Remember, this isn't a stray kitten we're dealing with – it's a literal dragon."

The dragon, apparently taking offence at being characterised as a potential menace, tilted its head and chirped softly, the sound carrying an almost musical quality that seemed designed to project that it was harmless. Its tail curled around its feet in a way that made it look smaller, more vulnerable.

"Don't give me that look," Kimberley muttered, crouching down to get a better look at their scaly problem. She reached out cautiously, her fingers stopping just short of touching its glimmering purple scales, which shifted through various jewel-toned hues under the flickering fluorescent light. "You're not going to torch the place the second we turn our backs, are you? Because I really can't afford to lose this job, and "dragon-related incident" probably isn't covered by our insurance."

The dragon flicked its tongue out, tasting the air like a snake, its amethyst eyes meeting hers with an unnervingly intelligent gaze that seemed to contain depths of understanding far beyond what any normal animal should possess. The intensity of its stare made Kimberley wonder, not for the first time, just how much it could comprehend.

Kimberley sighed heavily, sitting back on her heels and running a hand through her hair, loosening several strands from her already messy braid. "And now I'm talking to a dragon like it can actually answer me. Perfect. What a day this is turning out to be!"

Alice shuffled a few steps closer but maintained what she clearly considered a safe distance from the dragon, using her clipboard as a shield. "What if we call animal control? Or... I don't know, is there like a special department that deals with magical creatures? Like magical animal control or something?"

"Absolutely not," Kimberley said firmly, standing up and brushing her hands on her jeans with perhaps more vigour than necessary. "Have you seen the news stories about what happens to abandoned magical creatures? They end up in cages, or worse – dissected in some government lab. I'm not about to let that happen to this little guy, even if it did try to eat our paperwork."

Alice's brows knitted together in concern, her forehead creasing above her wire-rimmed glasses. "But we can't just keep it here! What if someone comes in and sees it? What if it freaks out and starts breaking things? Or worse – what if it starts a fire? We could all lose our jobs. Or die."

Kimberley crossed her arms, her eyes narrowing as she ran through their limited options in her head. Her shift was nearly over, and the store would be closing in a few hours. The dragon couldn't stay out on the sales floor – that much was blindingly obvious – but the back office wasn't exactly a long-term solution either. It was barely suitable for human occupation, let alone housing a magical creature with unknown needs and abilities.

Her gaze drifted to the office door, her mind racing through possibilities. If she locked it... maybe, just maybe, she could keep the dragon safely hidden until closing time. It wasn't an ideal solution by any means, but it would buy her enough time to finish her shift without the creature raising any alarm or causing a store-wide panic. And if she checked on it regularly, she could make sure it wasn't redecorating the office with scorch marks or turning important documents into a nest.

"Here's what we're going to do," Kimberley said, her tone shifting into what her co-workers called her "supervisor voice" – firm, confident, and brooking no argument. "We'll leave it here for now. At least that way it won't startle anybody. I'll lock the door so no one wanders in and gets the surprise of their life. And Alice…" She turned to the younger girl, levelling her with a serious look that she hoped conveyed the gravity of the situation. "You're not going to breathe a word about this to anyone. Not your co-workers, not your friends, not your social media followers. No one. Got it?"

Alice's eyes widened behind her glasses. "What? Why not? Shouldn't we at least tell *someone*?"

"The absolute last thing we need right now is a store full of panicked customers or gossiping co-workers," Kimberley replied, running a hand through her hair again in frustration. "You know how people are. The second they hear the word "dragon", they'll be texting their friends, taking pictures, posting on every social media platform known to humanity and making a scene. We don't need that kind of attention, and neither does our scaly friend here."

Alice hesitated, glancing at the dragon, which had given up its paper-eating adventures and was now curling up in a corner, its wings tucked tightly against its body like a leather jacket worn against the cold. It looked surprisingly small and vulnerable in that moment, its earlier defiance replaced by an almost puppy-like exhaustion that made Kimberley's heart twist despite her better judgment.

"Alright," Alice said finally, her voice heavy with reluctance. "I won't say anything. I promise."

"It's for the best," Kimberley said with a faint smile, grateful for the younger girl's co-operation despite her obvious reservations. "And don't worry – it's only until closing. Once the store's empty, I'll figure out what to do with our unexpected guest. Somehow."

Alice nodded, though her expression suggested she was already imagining all the ways this situation could go horrifically wrong. "Ok. But if this thing starts breathing fire or trying to eat more than just paper, I'm going home."

Kimberley nodded in agreement, unable to blame her for the caveat.

She crouched down once more, reaching out to the dragon with slow, deliberate movements. It lifted its head as she approached, its eyes watching her with an intensity that made her wonder again just how much intelligence lay behind that ethereal gaze. "Listen, little guy," she said softly, feeling only slightly ridiculous for talking to it like a child. "You're going to stay here for a bit, alright? No making a mess, no setting anything on fire, and definitely no eating any more paperwork. Got it?"

The dragon blinked slowly, then nudged its warm snout against her hand in what felt remarkably like agreement. Its scales were warm under her touch, smooth like sun-heated stones, and she could feel a gentle vibration running through its body that reminded her of a cat's purr.

Kimberley straightened up, brushing her hands on her jeans yet again, trying to shake off the lingering sensation of the dragon's supernatural warmth. "Alright. Time to lock you in here and hope for the best."

Satisfied that the dragon was settled in its makeshift sanctuary among the office debris, Kimberley closed the door and locked it with a decisive click, pocketing the key with a sense of finality that felt almost prophetic.

She turned to Alice, who was still lingering nearby, still clutching her clipboard like a shield against the strangeness of their situation. "Remember – not a word to anyone. This stays between us."

Alice held up her hands in mock surrender, clipboard and all. "My lips are sealed tighter than the break room microwave after someone heats up fish. But you'd better check on it every five minutes. I'm not taking the blame if something goes wrong. I've got student loans to pay off."

"Don't worry," Kimberley said, already heading back towards the sales floor where undoubtedly a dozen new crises awaited her attention. "I've got it under control. Probably. Maybe. We'll see."

As she walked away, the responsibility of the situation weighed heavily on her. The dragon was her problem now, whether she liked it or not, and she had a sinking feeling that this was just the beginning of what promised to be an incredibly complicated situation. At least retail had prepared her for expecting the unexpected – though she had to admit, "abandoned dragon in the back office" hadn't been on her list of potential workplace challenges when she'd started this job.

The real question now was what she would do with it after closing time. But that was a problem for future Kimberley. Present Kimberley still had several hours of regular retail chaos to manage.

Chapter Three

The sun had already dipped below the city's jagged skyline by the time Kimberley finally reached her apartment building, casting the bustling streets in a hazy orange glow that made everything look slightly surreal. She had managed to carry the dragon home by holding him safely tucked under her black leather jacket as she wore it, trying her best to look casual despite the occasional wiggle or warm puff of air against her ribs. The little creature had remained remarkably still during their journey, and she figured he must have been thoroughly exhausted after his eventful day of being abandoned and subsequently hidden in a retail store's back office. To her relief, the few people they passed had barely given her a second glance; dragons weren't exactly uncommon in the city – most were small, well-behaved creatures specifically bred for companionship – though they were far from ordinary pets.

"Alright, here we are," Kimberley muttered under her breath as she fumbled with her keys, finally managing to unlock the front door to her building. She glanced down at the dragon, which was now sniffing the air with obvious interest, its head tilted at an angle that somehow managed to convey both curiosity and judgment. "Don't freak out my neighbours, ok? The last thing I need is Mrs Henderson from 2B calling the building manager about unauthorised magical creatures."

The dragon responded with a quiet huff that might have been agreement or derision – it was hard to tell – but Kimberley's heart nearly stopped when a small puff of smoke curled from its nostrils, dancing in the evening air like a miniature ghost. She froze in place, her pulse racing as she watched the smoke dissipate into nothing, leaving no trace of its existence except her own rattled nerves.

"Cool it with the fire tricks," she whispered urgently, quickly ushering the dragon inside before anyone could notice. "I really don't want to be threatened with eviction over dragon-related incidents."

The apartment building was about as unremarkable as they came in this part of the city: beige walls that had probably been white at some point in the distant past, overhead lights that flickered with concerning irregularity, and a persistent smell of mildew that seemed to have taken up permanent residence despite countless complaints to maintenance. Kimberley carried the dragon up two flights of stairs to her unit, wincing at every sound that seemed to echo through the hallway. She found herself holding her breath each time they passed a neighbour's door, silently praying that no one would choose this moment to step out.

Once safely inside her apartment, she locked the door with perhaps more force than necessary and leaned against it, letting out a long sigh that seemed to carry the weight of her entire bizarre day. "Home sweet home," she said with a gesture that encompassed the modest living space, her voice carrying a mix of relief and resignation.

She carefully lowered the dragon to the floor, watching as it immediately began to explore its new surroundings. The creature padded forward with deliberate grace, its sharp, intelligent eyes scanning every detail of the space: the mismatched furniture she'd collected from various charity shops, the overcrowded bookshelves that threatened to collapse under the weight of her ever-growing collection, and the small kitchen area that optimistically doubled as a dining space despite barely having room for a folding table. The dragon let out a soft, musical trill, its tail swishing behind it in what Kimberley chose to interpret as approval rather than criticism.

"Yeah, it's not much," Kimberley admitted, dropping her worn messenger bag onto the couch with a heavy thud. "But it's definitely better than a fitting room floor or that disaster zone we call a back office. At least here you won't have to dodge old inventory reports and forgotten lunches."

The dragon continued its methodical inspection of its new territory, first sniffing at a pile of clean laundry she'd been meaning to fold for the past three days, then moving on to investigate the kitchen area with its collection of chipped mugs and mismatched appliances. Kimberley watched it warily, half-expecting it to start chewing on the cabinet doors or testing its fire-breathing capabilities against the curtains. But to her mounting surprise, it seemed more interested in careful exploration than chaos-causing, moving through the space with an almost scholarly attention to detail.

She reached up to rub the back of her neck, trying to massage away some of the tension while simultaneously attempting to figure out her next move. "Alright, first things first," she muttered to herself, falling back on her retail training of breaking big problems into smaller, manageable tasks. "What do dragons even eat? Because I'm pretty sure I can't just order pizza and hope for the best."

Grabbing her phone from her bag, she sank onto the couch and started scrolling through search results, her frown deepening with each unhelpful link. Most of the information seemed useless – generic care tips clearly written by people who had swapped the word "dog" for "dragon", dragons for sale, and advertisements for overpriced dragon chow sold by specialty pet shops that probably catered to rich people. She glanced at the dragon, which had found a spot by the window and was curled up like a cat.

"You don't exactly look like the type to eat kibble," Kimberley said thoughtfully, tapping her phone against her chin. "What are you, a steak kind of dragon? Or maybe you're more traditional – you know, eating gemstones like in those old stories my grandma used to tell?"

The dragon's head snapped up at the word "gemstones", its eyes gleaming with sudden interest that bordered on excitement. Kimberley raised an eyebrow, equal parts amused and concerned by the reaction.

"Seriously? Gems?" She made a show of glancing around her decidedly jewel-free apartment, as if she might suddenly discover a forgotten treasure trove hiding between the furniture. "Yeah, that's definitely not happening on my salary. You'll have to settle for something less... shiny. Unless you want to start paying rent, in which case we can discuss a gem-based diet."

She pushed herself up from the couch with a

grunt and opened the fridge, surveying its meagre contents with a critical eye. The interior light illuminated what could generously be called a bachelor's shopping list: milk that was probably still good, a half-empty bottle of orange juice she didn't remember buying, containers of leftover takeout in various states of questionable freshness, and a sad-looking bag of spinach that had long since given up on life. Not exactly a feast fit for a magical creature.

"Ok, let's try this," she said, extracting a piece of leftover chicken that looked and smelt safe enough. She crouched down and held it out cautiously, ready to pull back if necessary. "Are you hungry? Because this is pretty much all I've got unless you want to try your luck with the spinach."

The dragon sniffed the offered chicken with delicate interest, then snapped it up in one lightning-quick movement that made Kimberley yelp and jerk her hand back reflexively, her heart racing even though the creature's aim had been perfect.

"Alright, noted," she said, shaking her head as she straightened up. "Fast reflexes. Very fast reflexes. Good to know for future feeding times."

The dragon seemed thoroughly pleased with itself, licking its chops with obvious satisfaction before settling back into its spot with all the dignity of a creature that hadn't just nearly given its host a heart attack. Kimberley couldn't help but smile at its self-satisfied expression, already feeling herself growing dangerously attached to this strange, unexpected guest.

Her phone buzzed insistently on the coffee table, and she grabbed it without thinking, her mind still preoccupied with dragon dietary requirements. The name "Rai" lit up the screen like a neon sign, and Kimberley's stomach performed an impressive acrobatic routine as reality came crashing back.

"Hey," she answered, trying to keep her voice casual despite the sudden surge of panic in her chest.

"Hey, you," Rai's voice came through the speaker, warm and cheerful in a way that usually made Kimberley's heart flutter but now just added to her anxiety. "Are we still on for dinner tonight? I've been craving that new Thai place all day."

Kimberley froze in place, her eyes darting to the dragon lounging in her living area like it belonged there. She had completely forgotten about their dinner plans, the strangeness of the day having driven all normal arrangements from her mind.

"Uh, yeah," she said quickly, her brain scrambling for a plausible excuse that didn't involve magical creatures. "But, uh, can we do my place instead? Work was absolutely crazy today, and I'm too wiped to go out. Like, seriously wiped. The kind of tired where putting shoes on feels like climbing a mountain."

"Sure, no problem," Rai said, though there was a distinct note of curiosity in her tone that suggested she'd picked up on something being off. "Is everything ok? You sound a little... weird."

Kimberley hesitated, her eyes drifting back to the dragon, which had now opened one eye to watch her with what looked suspiciously like amusement. "Yeah," she said finally, trying to inject confidence into her voice. "Just... a really long day. I'll explain everything when you get here."

"Alright, if you say so. I'll grab some takeout and head over. Thai food in pyjamas sounds pretty perfect anyway. See you soon."

Kimberley hung up and immediately flopped back onto the couch, running both hands through her hair in a gesture of combined frustration and resignation. She had absolutely no idea how she was going to explain the presence of an abandoned dragon to Rai.

"Well," she said, looking at the dragon, which was now watching her with undisguised interest, "I guess you're meeting my girlfriend tonight. Try not to freak her out, ok? She's usually pretty chill, but this might be pushing it, even for her."

The dragon tilted its head at an angle that somehow managed to be both endearing and slightly mocking, letting out a soft trill that sounded suspiciously like laughter. Kimberley had a feeling the creature understood far more than it was letting on, which was both comforting and slightly unnerving.

"And definitely no fire-breathing," she added firmly, pointing a stern finger at the dragon. "I like this apartment, and more importantly, I really like my security deposit."

Chapter Four

Kimberley sat perched on the edge of her couch, one leg bouncing with nervous energy as she waited for Rai to arrive. Her eyes kept drifting to the dragon, which had settled comfortably into its corner spot, its amethyst scales catching the light. There was something mesmerising about the way the colours shifted and changed with each subtle movement, like watching the surface of a soap bubble. Despite the chaos of the day and the uncertainty of her current situation, Kimberley couldn't help but feel a sense of wonder at the creature's beauty. She found herself questioning, not for the first time, how anyone could abandon something so remarkable.

The thought of the dragon's abandonment led her mind inevitably back to Rai, and how she would react to seeing an unexpected magical creature in the flat. Kimberley's stomach performed another anxious flip. While Rai had always been understanding about most things, "surprise dragon" felt like it might be pushing the boundaries of even the most accommodating girlfriend's tolerance.

A knock at the door sent Kimberley's heart racing. She jumped up from the couch and shot the dragon a firm look. "Behave," she whispered urgently. "No fire, no smoke, no eating anything unless it's offered to you. Got it?"

The dragon blinked at her with what might have been agreement or might have been amusement – it was still hard to tell. Taking a deep breath, Kimberley opened the door to reveal exactly who she expected: Rai, her girlfriend of eight months, looking as striking as ever despite clearly having come straight from her job at the city library.

Rai was the kind of person who turned heads without trying, though she seemed perpetually unaware of the effect she had on people. Her warm brown skin seemed to glow in the hallway's fluorescent lighting, and her mass of dark curls had been gathered into a casual updo that somehow managed to look both effortlessly elegant and slightly dishevelled. She wore wire-rimmed glasses that gave her an academic air, which was enhanced by her habit of dressing like someone who'd raided a very stylish professor's closet – today it was an oversized cardigan in deep burgundy over a crisp white shirt, paired with high-waisted trousers and comfortable but fashionable flats. A small constellation of freckles dusted her nose and cheeks, and her full lips were curved in their usual gentle smile.

She was also, Kimberley noted with both amusement and mild concern, completely focused on the numerous bags of Thai takeout she was carrying. The scent of sesame oil and spices wafted through the doorway, making Kimberley's stomach growl despite her anxiety.

"I might have gone a little overboard," Rai admitted as she made her way to the kitchen area, her attention still fixed on not dropping any of the containers. "But I couldn't decide what to get, and you sounded like you needed comfort food."

Kimberley watched with growing amazement as Rai bustled around the small kitchen, completely oblivious to the magical creature lounging just metres away. It was a testament to both Rai's focus on her task and the dragon's surprisingly good behaviour that the situation felt almost normal – well, as normal as having a magical creature in the flat could be.

Their relationship had always been like this in some ways – comfortable and easy, with Rai accepting things about Kimberley that might have sent others running. Even Kimberley's subtle hints about her magical abilities had been met with casual acceptance rather than fear or judgment. Being a witch wasn't something Kimberley advertised – she kept her magic small and unobtrusive, more useful than flashy – and Rai, being firmly in the non-magical portion of the population, had never pressed for more details than Kimberley was willing to share. It was one of the many things Kimberley loved about her.

This is actually kind of perfect, Kimberley thought, watching Rai methodically unpack their dinner. The dragon was being remarkably well-behaved, curled up quietly in its corner as if it understood the importance of making a good first impression. The fact that Rai hadn't immediately noticed it felt like a good sign – surely if it was going to be dangerous or aggressive, it would have made its presence known by now.

Just as Rai was carefully transferring a handful of prawn crackers into one of Kimberley's mismatched bowls, she happened to glance up. Her eyes widened comically behind her glasses, and the crackers scattered across the counter as her hands went slack with surprise.

"Oh my God!" Rai uttered under her breath, abandoning the food entirely and moving towards the living area with careful, measured steps. Her face lit up with pure delight as she sank onto the couch, extending her hand towards the dragon. "Hello there, beautiful."

To Kimberley's absolute astonishment, Rai patted her lap invitingly, as casual as if she was calling over a house cat. Even more surprising was the dragon's reaction – it practically bounded across the room, all previous dignity forgotten in its enthusiasm to reach Rai. The creature that had spent most of the day being cautious and reserved was suddenly acting like an excited puppy, making small trilling sounds of joy as it climbed onto Rai's lap.

"I can't believe you've got a dragon!" Rai exclaimed, running her hands over the creature's scales with obvious expertise. "Oh, you're absolutely gorgeous, aren't you? Look at these markings – definitely some forest dragon ancestry in there. You can tell by the way the scales pattern along the spine."

Kimberley stood frozen between the kitchen and living areas, holding a container of pad Thai and trying to process this unexpected turn of events. "You know about dragons?"

Rai looked up with a bright smile, still scratching under the dragon's chin in exactly the right spot if its blissful expression was anything to go by. "Oh yeah! My cousin had one when we were kids. Smaller than this fellow, but similar colouring. Dragons are fascinating creatures – so intelligent, so misunderstood. People think they're just pets or novelties, but they're remarkably complex beings."

Kimberley felt a weight lift from her shoulders as she finished plating their food. She carried everything to the coffee table and set it down. She sat on the couch next to Rai, passing her a bowl of noodles. Rai accepted it with a grateful smile, cradling it in her hands while simultaneously maintaining dragon-petting duties with impressive skill.

"Here," Rai said, offering the dragon a small piece of chicken from her bowl. "This is perfect for you. But no chilli sauce – spicy food makes dragons hiccup fire. I learnt that the hard way when I was twelve. My aunt's curtains never really recovered." She glanced at Kimberley with a grin. "They can have plain noodles and rice too, but meat is best for maintaining healthy scales. Also, the protein helps with strength."

The dragon accepted each offered morsel with impeccable manners, its earlier speed-eating apparently replaced by proper dinner etiquette. Kimberley found herself falling a little bit more in love with both the dragon and Rai as she watched them interact, her heart warming at the way Rai praised the creature's gentle behaviour between bites of her own dinner.

Once the food was finished and the dishes were cleared away – a task Kimberley handled while Rai continued her dragon-bonding session – Kimberley settled back onto the couch, ready to explain the day's events. The dragon remained contentedly sprawled across Rai's lap, occasionally making small sounds of happiness when she found particularly good scratching spots.

Kimberley launched into the story of her extraordinarily unusual day at work. When she reached the part about the punk woman in the changing rooms, Rai suddenly sat up straighter, her expression shifting from contentment to concern.

"Kim, wait," she said, gently tilting the dragon's head. "Look at this – there's something in his ear."

Kimberley leaned closer, squinting at where Rai was pointing. Sure enough, there was something that looked like a tattoo on the dragon's inner ear, small black letters that had been partially hidden by the creature's natural markings: *Romco Labs. No. 39.*

"Romco Labs?" Kimberley repeated, the words leaving a bad taste in her mouth. Something about the clinical nature of the marking made her skin crawl.

Rai was already pulling out her phone, her fingers flying over the screen. Her frown deepened as she scrolled through search results. "It's a research facility on the industrial estate," she said, her voice tight with growing anger. "They do testing on dragons. There are dozens of complaints about animal cruelty, but they keep operating because they're technically within legal guidelines." She turned the phone so Kimberley could see the reviews – a litany of one-star ratings and horror stories from former employees.

"Number thirty-nine," Kimberley muttered, reaching out to stroke the dragon's head. "That's not an address or a building number, is it?"

"No," Rai confirmed grimly, pulling the dragon closer as if to protect it. "I think it's his designation. Like... like he was just a number to them."

The dragon made a small sound, almost like a whimper, and pressed its head against Rai's hand. The gesture was so human, so vulnerable, that Kimberley felt her throat tighten with emotion. Suddenly, the punk woman's story about the dragon being "nothing but trouble" took on a darker meaning. Had she been involved with the lab? Had it been her job to dispose of the dragon when they were done with whatever tests they'd been running? Or had the dragon fallen into her incapable hands some other way? Perhaps it was one of many animals from the rescue system, another case where an adoption hadn't worked out.

As if reading Kimberley's thoughts, Rai looked up with fierce determination in her eyes. "He's not going back there," she said firmly. "Whatever happened at that lab, whatever they were doing to him – it's over now. Right?"

Kimberley nodded, reaching out to scratch the dragon's chin. "Right," she agreed, even as her mind raced with the possibility that someone out there still believed they had a legal claim to the dragon. "He's safe now."

The dragon looked between them with those intelligent amethyst eyes, and Kimberley could have sworn she saw gratitude in its gaze. Whatever complications this situation might bring, whatever consequences might come from their discovery, she knew they'd made the right choice. Some things were worth the risk.

54

Chapter Five

Sunlight filtered through the gaps in Kimberley's curtains, painting stripes of golden warmth across the rumpled bedding. She lay on her side, watching Rai's peaceful face on the pillow next to her, admiring the way the morning light caught the edges of her curls and turned them into a soft halo. The peaceful silence of early Sunday morning wrapped around them like the comfortable duvet, broken only by the quiet sounds of the city waking up outside and the gentle, rhythmic breathing of the dragon curled up at the foot of the bed.

Rai's eyes fluttered open, and a slow smile spread across her face as she met Kimberley's gaze. "Morning," she murmured, her voice still rough with sleep. "How long have you been awake?"

"Not long," Kimberley whispered back, mindful of their sleeping guest. "I can't believe how well he slept. No fire-breathing, no midnight wandering, just... curled up there like he's done it a thousand times before."

They both shifted carefully to look at the dragon, which remained peacefully asleep, its amethyst scales catching the morning light and throwing tiny purple reflections across the ceiling. Its wings were tucked neatly against its body, and its tail was curled protectively around itself, the tip twitching occasionally as it dreamed.

"He probably hasn't had many chances to sleep somewhere safe," Rai said softly, her expression clouding with concern. "Those reviews I found about Romco Labs... some of them mentioned the dragons being kept in small cages. Metal cages." She practically spat the last words, her usual gentleness giving way to anger. "Can you imagine? Keeping a creature like that locked up in a metal box?"

Kimberley reached out to squeeze Rai's hand, trying to offer comfort even as her own stomach churned at the thought. "No wonder he seems so grateful for basic kindness. A proper bed must feel like luxury after that."

Rai was quiet for a moment, her thumb absently stroking the back of Kimberley's hand as she seemed lost in thought. "You know," she said finally, her voice taking on that particular tone that Kimberley had learnt to associate with potentially questionable ideas, "it's Sunday."

"Yes, that's generally what comes after Saturday," Kimberley agreed, raising an eyebrow. "Your point?"

"The lab might be closed, or at least operating with minimal staff." Rai propped herself up on one elbow, her eyes bright with purpose. "We could go and take a look. Try to figure out what they were doing to him, maybe find some information that could help us understand what he's been through."

Kimberley felt her chest tighten with anxiety. "You mean break into the lab? That doesn't sound like a fantastic Sunday plan to me."

"Not break in," Rai clarified quickly, though her expression suggested she might not be entirely opposed to that idea either. "Just… a bit of exploration. We could walk past it, see what the place looks like from the outside. Maybe peek through some windows if we get the chance. Don't you want to know more about where he came from?"

The dragon chose that moment to wake up, lifting its head and regarding them both with those impossibly intelligent eyes. It let out a small trill that sounded almost like a question, its head tilted in a way that made Kimberley's resolve crumble slightly.

"It would be trespassing," she said, but her protest sounded weak even to her own ears. "And what if it upsets him? Being back near that place?"

Rai sat up fully, the covers pooling around her waist. "We don't have to get too close. And we'll watch him carefully – if he shows any signs of distress, we'll reassure him, let him know that he's safe now. But Kim, what if there are others like him in there? Don't we have a responsibility to at least try to find out what's going on?"

Kimberley groaned, pressing her face into her pillow. She knew that tone in Rai's voice –

that mix of determination and moral conviction that made it nearly impossible to argue against her. And worse, she knew Rai was right. The mystery of the lab and what they might have done to their dragon guest had been gnawing at her since they'd discovered that clinical tattoo in his ear.

"Fine," she muttered into the pillow before lifting her head to fix Rai with a stern look. "But we're just looking. No breaking and entering, no confronting anyone, no heroic rescue missions. Got it?"

Rai's face lit up with a brilliant smile, and she leaned over to press a quick kiss to Kimberley's forehead. "Got it. Totally innocent Sunday walk that just happens to take us past a questionable research facility. Nothing suspicious about that at all."

The dragon watched their exchange with what looked suspiciously like amusement, its tail swishing back and forth across the bedding. When Kimberley caught its eye, she could have sworn it winked at her.

"Breakfast first," she insisted, pushing herself up and swinging her legs over the side of the bed. "If we're going to do something potentially stupid, we should at least do it on full stomachs."

They moved through their morning routine with practiced ease, working around each other in Kimberley's small bathroom and kitchen as if they'd been doing it for years instead of months. The dragon sat close by on top of the small dining table, watching their preparations with obvious interest and accepting offered bits of breakfast with impeccable manners.

"You're sure about this?" Kimberley asked one last time as she helped the dragon settle into its now-familiar position under her jacket. The creature's warm weight against her ribs felt oddly comforting, like wearing a living hot water bottle.

"Absolutely," Rai confirmed, shouldering her worn leather messenger bag – the kind that seemed mandatory for librarians – and checking that her phone was fully charged. "The industrial estate is on the other side of the city, but we can take the bus most of the way. It'll look less suspicious than taking a taxi."

Kimberley locked her apartment door, trying to ignore the voice in her head that kept insisting this was a terrible idea. The dragon shifted slightly under her jacket, pressing closer as if offering reassurance.

"Right," she said, falling into step beside Rai as they made their way down the stairs. "Just a normal Sunday morning walk to a potentially evil laboratory. What could possibly go wrong?"

The dragon made a small huffing sound, and Kimberley couldn't help but smile despite her anxiety. Whatever they found at Romco Labs, at least they were in it together.

***

The industrial estate sprawled before them like an abandoned movie set, all concrete and corrugated metal under a bleached sky. Their footsteps echoed with a hollow resonance off the buildings as they walked, the sound bouncing between walls in a way that made the space feel even more desolate. The usual weekday bustle of delivery trucks and workers had been replaced by an eerie silence that made every small noise seem significant.

"It has to be around here somewhere," Rai muttered, consulting her phone for what felt like the hundredth time. The screen showed a satellite view of the area, but the buildings all looked identical from above – featureless rectangles arranged in neat rows like pieces on a giant's chess board.

Kimberley adjusted her jacket, careful not to disturb the dragon too much. He had been unusually still during their journey, nothing like his curious self from yesterday. She could feel tension radiating from his small body, and occasionally a tremor would run through him that made her heart ache.

"Maybe we should go home," she suggested softly, worried about the dragon's increasing distress. "We can come back another time, or find another way to..."

She broke off as the dragon suddenly went rigid against her side, its body stiffening like a coiled spring before it began to shake violently. Following its terrified gaze, she found herself looking at a building that appeared largely identical to its neighbours – grey walls, high windows, metal doors – except for a small, professionally designed sign next to the entrance: *Romco Laboratories – Advancing Dragon Research.*

"This is it," Rai whispered, her hand finding Kimberley's and squeezing tight. "Look at how he's reacting. He knows this place."

They approached cautiously, keeping close to the wall as they made their way to one of the windows. The glass was tinted, but they could still make out shapes in the darkness beyond – the clinical outline of laboratory equipment, rows of metal tables, and something that made Kimberley's stomach turn: stacks of cages, their bars casting long shadows across the floor.

"The reviews weren't exaggerating," Rai said, her voice tight with anger. She pressed her face closer to the glass, shielding her eyes with her hands to see better. "Those cages... they're barely big enough for them to turn around in."

The dragon whimpered softly, burrowing deeper into Kimberley's jacket as if trying to hide from the mere sight of its former prison. She stroked its side gently through the fabric, trying to offer what comfort she could.

"We need to get inside," Rai said suddenly, turning to face Kimberley with fierce determination in her eyes. "We need to see exactly what they're doing here."

Kimberley bit her lip, glancing around the empty estate. Her magic tingled under her skin, responding to her emotions even before she'd made a conscious decision. She rarely used it for anything more significant than discreetly warming up cold coffee or finding lost keys. The thought of using it to break into a building felt like crossing a line she'd always been careful to maintain.

But then the dragon trembled against her again, and she remembered that tattoo in its ear: number thirty-nine – just a number to the people who had imprisoned it here.

"Ok," she said quietly, already reaching out with her magic to feel for security systems. "Stand back a little."

She closed her eyes, letting her awareness expand beyond her physical senses. The building's security system revealed itself to her magical perception like a web of glowing threads – cameras, motion sensors, electronic locks all interconnected in a complex pattern. It wasn't particularly sophisticated; clearly, they relied more on the isolation of the location than high-tech security.

Kimberley took a deep breath and began to work, her fingers moving in subtle gestures as she carefully manipulated the threads of energy. One by one, she disabled the cameras, convinced the motion sensors to ignore their presence, and finally, with a soft click that seemed impossibly loud in the Sunday silence, unlocked the door.

"That's... not something I knew you could do," Rai said, watching with wide eyes as Kimberley pushed the door open.

"It's not something I make a habit of doing," Kimberley replied grimly, ushering Rai inside before quickly closing the door behind them. "But this feels like a worthy exception."

The interior of the lab was even worse than what they'd glimpsed through the windows. Harsh fluorescent emergency lights cast a sickly glow over everything, creating deep shadows that seemed to pulse with remembered pain. The air was thick with the sharp smell of disinfectant barely masking something else – something that made Kimberley think of fear and suffering.

The dragon was shaking constantly now, making small sounds of distress that tore at Kimberley's heart. She stroked its head through her jacket, murmuring soft words of comfort. "It's ok, you're safe. We won't let them hurt you again. We're just here to look, and then we'll go home."

Rai moved through the space like a ghost, her usual animated energy replaced by horrified focus as she documented everything with her phone's camera. The cages they'd seen from outside were even smaller up close, barely large enough for an adult dragon to lie down. Many showed signs of desperate attempts at escape – deep scratches gouged into the bars and scorch marks from fire breath.

"Look at this," Rai called softly, standing by a desk covered in papers. Her hands shook as she leafed through them. "They were testing different methods of suppressing fire production. Forcing them to breathe fire until they were exhausted, then... then testing how long it took them to recover under different conditions."

Kimberley joined her, still cradling the trembling dragon. The papers were full of clinical language that tried to disguise cruelty as science: *Subject showed marked distress during trials. Recovery time increased significantly under pressure conditions. Test terminated when subject became non-responsive.*

They moved deeper into the lab, each discovery worse than the last. There was a room full of treadmills fitted with shock plates to force exhausted dragons to keep running. Another contained tanks of water where they had apparently tested how long dragons could hold their breath. Everywhere they looked, they found evidence of suffering disguised as research.

"This can't be legal," Rai whispered, tears streaming down her face as she photographed another set of documents. "They're sentient beings, not lab equipment."

The dragon suddenly let out a high-pitched whine, drawing their attention to a door they hadn't noticed before. Through the window, they could see rows of occupied cages, each containing a dragon in varying states of distress. Some of the smaller ones paced their tiny spaces restlessly, while others lay curled and defeated, their once-bright scales dulled by captivity.

"Oh God," Kimberley uttered, her own tears falling freely now.

She wanted desperately to help them, to throw open every cage even if it meant only being able to lead just a few to freedom. But she knew she couldn't – not today, not like this. Any evidence of a break-in would put the facility on high alert, making it harder to help every last dragon in the long run.

"We have to go," she said finally, her voice rough with emotion. "We have what we need – proof of what they're doing. I want to help them all. We *will* help them all. But we have to be smart about it."

Rai nodded reluctantly, her phone clutched tight in her hand. "We'll come back for them," she promised, both to herself and to the dragons watching them with desperate eyes. "We'll find a way to get this place shut down."

They made their way back through the lab, each step made difficult by the knowledge of what they were leaving behind. At the door, Kimberley paused to reset the security systems and relock everything, ensuring no trace of their visit remained. Her magic felt bitter in her mouth, tainted by the horrors they'd witnessed.

The dragon in her jacket had gone quiet, but she could feel its rapid heartbeat against her ribs. As they emerged into the harsh sunlight, she pulled it closer, trying to pour all her love and protection into the gesture.

"Never again," she whispered fiercely as they walked away from the facility, unable to look back at the building that housed so much suffering. "They're never going to hurt you again. I promise."

Rai's hand found hers, squeezing tight. "We'll give him everything they didn't – space, good food, comfort, love. And we'll find a way to help the others too. Whatever it takes."

The dragon made a soft sound, somewhere between a whimper and a trill, and pressed closer to Kimberley. She thought about his peaceful sleep at the foot of her bed that morning, how content he'd looked in the sunlight. Every creature deserved that kind of peace, that sense of safety. The fact that someone could look at these remarkable beings and see only test subjects made her blood boil.

As they walked back towards the bus stop, both still wiping away tears, Kimberley's mind was already racing with plans. They had evidence now – proof of the cruelty happening behind those walls. It wouldn't be easy to bring down a research facility, but they had to try. For the dragon in her arms, for all the others still trapped in those cages, they had to find a way to make this right.

Chapter Six

The walk back to Kimberley's flat felt longer than usual, the mood heavy with memories of what they'd witnessed at Romco Labs. Neither of them spoke much during the journey, both lost in their own thoughts as the dragon remained unusually still and quiet beneath Kimberley's jacket. The cheerful weekend bustle of the city seemed almost offensive after what they'd seen – how could everyone be going about their normal Sunday activities when such cruelty existed just a few miles away?

As soon as they were safely inside the apartment, Kimberley carefully extracted the dragon from her jacket. The creature's usual grace was absent as it stumbled slightly, clearly exhausted from the emotional strain of returning to its former prison. Its amethyst scales had lost some of their lustre, appearing dull and lifeless under the apartment's lighting.

"Here," Rai said softly, already arranging cushions in the corner by the window – the spot the dragon had claimed as its own the day before. "Let's get you comfortable."

The dragon allowed itself to be guided to the makeshift nest, curling up tightly with its tail wrapped protectively around itself. Its eyes remained open, watching them with an intensity that spoke of lingering fear, as if afraid they might disappear and leave it alone.

"I'll make us a cup of tea," Kimberley announced, needing something practical to do with her hands. She moved to the kitchen on autopilot, filling the kettle and pulling out mugs while Rai continued to comfort the dragon, speaking to it in low, soothing tones.

The familiar ritual of tea-making helped ground her somewhat – measuring loose leaves into the infuser, waiting for the water to boil, arranging cookies on a plate because they all deserved something sweet after the morning they'd had. When she returned to the living area with the laden tray, Rai was sitting cross-legged on the floor next to the dragon, gently stroking its head.

"He's trembling," Rai reported quietly, accepting a mug of tea with her free hand. "I can't even imagine what he must have gone through in that terrible place."

Kimberley settled down beside them, positioning the plate of cookies within easy reach. "At least now we know why he was so appreciative of a safe place to sleep. Those cages..." She broke off, her throat tightening at the memory.

They sat in silence for a while, sipping their tea and occasionally offering cookies to the dragon, who accepted them with none of its usual enthusiasm. The afternoon sun slanted through the window, creating pools of warmth on the floor that would normally have attracted the dragon's attention, but it remained curled tightly in its corner.

"We have to do something," Rai finally said, her voice firm despite its quietness. "We can't just leave them there."

Kimberley nodded slowly, cradling her warm mug between her hands. "I know. But what? We can't exactly break in and free them all – where would they go? We barely have room for one dragon, let alone..." She trailed off, remembering the rows of occupied cages they'd seen.

"There must be someone we can report this to," Rai mused, reaching for another cookie. "Some authority that oversees magical creature welfare? The evidence is right here." She patted her bag, which contained her phone full of damning photographs.

"But what if they don't care?" Kimberley's voice was bitter. "Those reviews you found – people have complained before, right? And nothing's changed. What if we report it and they just... ignore it? Or worse, what if they warn the lab and they hide the evidence? Move the dragons somewhere else?"

The dragon made a soft, distressed sound, and they both immediately reached out to comfort it. Its scales were warming slightly under their touch, some of the earlier tension gradually easing from its body.

"We could try to find homes for them first," Rai suggested, though she didn't sound entirely convinced. "People who would be willing to take them in, like we did. Then once we have safe places lined up…"

"Break in and stage a massive dragon rescue?" Kimberley finished, raising an eyebrow. "That sounds like something that could go wrong in about a thousand different ways. Plus, it's definitely illegal."

"More illegal than what they're doing to those dragons?" Rai challenged, though her tone was more tired than argumentative.

Kimberley sighed, running a hand through her hair. "No, of course not. But us getting arrested won't help anyone. We'd need somewhere to keep them all safely while finding homes, money for food and care, probably veterinary help for some of them…" She gestured around her small apartment. "This isn't exactly a dragon sanctuary."

"I know," Rai admitted, deflating slightly. "I just keep thinking about them in those cages, waiting for the next experiment. It makes me feel sick that we just left them there."

The dragon lifted its head at her words, regarding them both with those impossibly intelligent eyes. It made a soft trilling sound that somehow managed to convey both understanding and gratitude, as if it knew they were trying to help its kind.

"Maybe we're thinking about this wrong," Kimberley said slowly, reaching out to scratch under the dragon's chin. "Instead of choosing between legal and illegal options, maybe we need to find a middle ground. Someone who has the resources and authority to help, but who would actually care enough to do something about it."

Rai nodded thoughtfully, finishing her tea. "That makes sense. We just need to figure out who that might be." She glanced at her phone, checking the time. "But maybe not tonight. We're exhausted, and I don't think we're in the right headspace to make good decisions right now."

As if to emphasise her point, the dragon yawned, showing off rows of delicate teeth before settling its head back down. Some of its natural colour was returning, the amethyst scales beginning to shimmer faintly in the late afternoon light.

"You're right," Kimberley agreed, collecting their empty mugs. "We should sleep on it. Maybe something will come to us in the morning." She paused, looking at Rai. "Stay over again? I think he feels safer with both of us here, and I need you too."

Rai smiled, soft and tired but genuine. "Of course. I might need to borrow some clothes though."

"Take your pick," said Kimberley. "I've got plenty here."

They spent the rest of the evening in quiet reflection, all three still processing the day's events. The dragon gradually relaxed, nibbling on small pieces of chicken from their dinner with growing enthusiasm. It even managed to doze off in short bursts, though it often startled awake, as if to check that they were still there.

As they prepared for bed that night, Kimberley found herself watching the dragon –their dragon, she realised, because somewhere in the past two days, it had become theirs to protect and care for. It was already curled up at the foot of the bed, its half-lidded eyes fixed on them as if to make sure they weren't going anywhere. Kimberley glanced at Rai, who met her gaze with a gentle smile.

"I think we all need this tonight," Rai said quietly, nodding towards the dragon.

Kimberley nodded in agreement. "Yeah. It's probably better if we keep it close. For all our sakes."

The dragon trilled softly, as though it understood, and Kimberley couldn't help but feel a little lighter knowing none of them would be sleeping alone tonight.

"We'll figure something out," Rai whispered, wrapping her arms around Kimberley from behind. "For all of them. We just need to be smart about it."

Kimberley leaned back into the embrace, drawing comfort from Rai's presence. "I know we will. We have to." She thought about all the dragons still trapped in those cages, waiting in the darkness of the lab. "Whatever it takes, we'll find a way to help them."

Chapter Seven

The next day, warm afternoon sunlight cascaded through the window of Kimberley's flat, casting long golden bars across the worn carpet. The light caught and refracted off the dragon's amethyst scales as it perched next to her on the couch, creating miniature purple prisms that danced across the wall. Kimberley shifted position, trying to find a more comfortable spot as she balanced her laptop on her knees, its fan whirring softly as she clicked through article after article. Her coffee table had become a makeshift research station, covered in notebooks filled with her increasingly messy handwriting – observations, theories, and half-formed plans crowding the pages.

She glanced at the time displayed in the corner of her screen and felt a flutter of anticipation – mid-afternoon already. She couldn't wait for Rai to get back from work so she could finally share the intricate plan she had spent hours piecing together like a complex puzzle.

The dragon, sensing her momentary distraction, let out a melodious trill and hopped closer, its claws making tiny scraping sounds against the fabric of the couch. Kimberley couldn't help but chuckle at its eagerness for attention, leaning forward to give it a gentle scratch under its delicate chin. The scales there were softer, more flexible, and warm to the touch.

"You're getting as impatient as I am, aren't you?" she murmured affectionately. "Don't worry, little one. She'll be here soon enough."

The creature tilted its head at the sound of her voice, its large, jewel-like eyes tracking her movements with an intelligence that still took her breath away. As Kimberley stood and stretched, feeling the stiffness in her muscles from sitting too long, she decided to take a break. Walking to the small kitchen area, its countertops cluttered with mugs and the remains of her hurried breakfast, she opened the fridge and was surprised to find an unopened packet of cooked chicken. A warm smile spread across her face as realisation dawned. Rai must have popped out to the corner shop for them before heading to work, thoughtful as ever, probably tiptoeing around to avoid disturbing Kimberley's sleep. The gesture made her heart swell with affection.

With careful fingers, she tore off several small pieces of the chicken and arranged them on a clean plate, watching as the dragon immediately perked up at the scent. It scuttled forward eagerly, its tail swishing with excitement as it began to eat with delicate precision. Kimberley leaned against the counter, observing the creature with a mixture of wonder and fondness. It amazed her how quickly the dragon had come to trust them, how its initially anxious demeanour – from when she had seen it being chastised and abandoned by its horrible ex-owner in her work's changing room – had transformed into this playful, affectionate personality. As it nibbled at the chicken, occasionally glancing up as if to make sure she was still there, Kimberley found herself reflecting on how bringing it home had been the right thing to do.

Her contemplation was interrupted by a familiar pattern of knocks at the door. Kimberley's heart leapt at the sound, and she quickly wiped her hands on a paper towel. "Rai!"

Opening the door revealed her girlfriend's bright smile, and Kimberley felt the tension she'd been carrying all day begin to ease.

"I managed to get off early," Rai explained, stepping inside and shrugging off her coat to reveal a chic, tailored blazer paired with a slim-fitting blouse that she had borrowed from Kimberley, wearing it in her own style. Her curls of dark hair were coming loose from their practical bun, and she smelt faintly of espresso and vanilla. "I couldn't focus properly – I've been thinking about this little one all day." She knelt down, and the dragon immediately abandoned its meal, chirping excitedly as it fluttered up to perch on her shoulder, nuzzling against her neck. Rai laughed softly at the greeting. "Seems like someone missed me too."

The sight made Kimberley's affection for both of them surge. "Your thoughtfulness shows," she said warmly, nodding towards the kitchen. "Thanks for dropping off the chicken earlier. You didn't have to do that."

Rai's cheeks coloured slightly as she waved away the thanks, her free hand reaching up to stroke the dragon's head. "It was nothing, really. I just figured you'd need something to keep him properly fed. The last thing we need is a hungry dragon making a mess of your flat."

Kimberley grinned as she moved to fill the kettle, the familiar routine of making tea helping to calm her nerves about the conversation ahead. "Well, I've got something important to tell you. Let's sit and talk it through over a cup of tea."

A few minutes later, they were settled on the couch, steaming mugs warming their hands. The dragon had made itself comfortable between them, occasionally stealing curious glances at their serious faces.

Kimberley took a deep breath, her mind thrumming with barely contained determination as she prepared to share what she'd uncovered. "I've been researching all day – digging through news archives, forums, social media, anything I could find. It turns out we're not the first ones who want to see the end of Romco Labs. There have been animal rights groups, environmental organisations, even a former employee turned whistleblower. But nothing's worked. Nobody with any real power seems to care, or if they do, they're not willing to act. It's like the urgency of the situation just... doesn't register with them. They can't – or won't – see what's really happening behind those walls."

Rai's expression darkened, her fingers tightening around her mug. "That's so infuriating," she said, her voice taut with anger. "But honestly? It doesn't surprise me. Big companies like that, they've got too many people in their pockets. Too much money at stake."

"Exactly," Kimberley agreed, leaning forward intently. "Which is precisely why I think we need to take matters into our own hands – work outside their rigged system entirely. I've been thinking about it all day, turning it over and over in my mind. We could get into the lab, just like we did yesterday, and free them all. Every last one. I can disable their security systems, just like before – the alarms, the cameras, everything. We could do this, Rai. We could actually do this."

Rai blinked rapidly, her expression cycling through amazement, concern, and something that looked like growing excitement. "Wait – you're actually serious about this? Kimberley, that's... that's incredible. And terrifying. But what happens after we get them out? Where would we even take them all? From what we saw, there must be dozens of dragons in there."

Kimberley's eyes sparkled with enthusiasm as she shared the other crucial piece of her plan. "That's the other thing I discovered. There's a dragon sanctuary in a city about fifty miles from here – they specifically work with dragons rescued from captivity, helping to rehabilitate them. We'd need someone to drive a van, someone we can trust, but once we get the dragons there, the sanctuary will take them in. They've done it before, helped with other rescue situations."

Rai's eyes widened, hope beginning to override her initial scepticism. "Are you certain they'll take them? All of them? No questions asked?"

"I'm confident," Kimberley replied, her voice firm. "And just in case Romco might think to try claiming the dragons legally afterwards, I can use my magic during the transport to remove their identity tattoos. That way, there's no way to track them or prove they belonged to the lab. They'll be free, truly free."

Rai took a deep breath through her nose, her teeth chewing at her lower lip as she processed everything. "That's... brilliant. Actually brilliant. But Kimberley, it's so risky. If we get caught..."

Kimberley hesitated, then admitted, "I am scared. Of course I am. The thought of what could happen if it all goes wrong is terrifying. But I'm more determined than scared. I can't just sit back and do nothing, not after what we witnessed in that hellhole yesterday. Those dragons, suffering in those tiny cages... If we plan this properly, time it right, use my magic to our advantage – no one will ever know it was us. We can make this work."

Rai nodded slowly, and Kimberley could see her girlfriend's resolve hardening, her shoulders squaring. "You're right. It is worth the risk. Every single second those dragons stay in that lab is another second of suffering we could have prevented. I'm with you, Kimberley. All the way."

Kimberley felt a wave of relief and gratitude wash over her, nearly making her eyes sting with tears. "We'll need to find a driver first – someone we can trust completely. And sort out a van, of course. Once we have those pieces in place, we can plan the timing down to the minute."

"I'll start thinking about who we could ask," Rai said, her mind clearly already racing through possibilities. "It has to be someone reliable. Someone who'll understand why this matters so much – and someone who can keep their mouth shut afterwards."

"I agree," Kimberley said firmly. "And the sooner we can arrange it, the better. Those dragons have suffered long enough."

They sat together in contemplative silence for a moment. The dragon, perhaps sensing the importance of their conversation, let out a soft, almost musical coo and pressed itself against Kimberley's knee. She reached down to stroke its warm scales, exchanging a meaningful glance with Rai. In that moment, she could see her own determination mirrored in her girlfriend's eyes, and it strengthened her resolve even further.

The plan carried risks that made her stomach clench when she thought about them for too long. But it was the only way forward that she could live with – and looking at the trust in the dragon's eyes, feeling Rai's steadfast support beside her, Kimberley knew they were ready to see it through.

Chapter Eight

The hum of the city outside Kimberley's flat was a distant murmur, almost drowned out by the whirr of her laptop fan and the soft scratching of her pen against paper as she added another potential contact to her growing list. Her cup of tea had long since gone cold, forgotten in the intensity of her search. The dragon watched her from its perch on a cushion nearby, its amethyst scales catching the warm lamplight as it tracked her increasingly agitated movements with concerned eyes.

Kimberley's leg bounced anxiously as she scrolled through yet another page of classified ads, her vision beginning to blur from staring at the screen for so long. Forum posts and unanswered emails cluttered her browser tabs, each one a frustrating dead end. Still no one. Still no van. She and Rai hadn't managed to think of a suitable person for the job, and desperation was creeping in. Kimberley had even started considering hiring a van herself – a daunting prospect, given she hadn't driven a car in years, let alone a vehicle as large as a van. She ran her fingers through her hair, disturbing the messy bun she'd hastily pulled it into hours ago.

"We're running out of time," she murmured into the quiet room, glancing at the dragon. Its scales glimmered with an almost phosphorescent quality as it tilted its head in response, sensing her unease. The gesture was so endearing, so perfectly attuned to her emotional state, that Kimberley couldn't help but reach out to scratch its chin, finding a moment of calm in the dragon's presence. "We'll figure it out," she promised, more to herself than the creature, though its gentle trill suggested it understood her words.

A sudden, sharp knock at the door shattered her thoughts, making her jump. She wasn't expecting anyone. The dragon perked up instantly, its entire body seeming to vibrate with excitement as it let out a soft, encouraging noise. Kimberley stood carefully, her legs slightly unsteady from sitting so long. The carpet muffled her footsteps as she crossed the room, and she found herself holding her breath as she leaned forward to peer through the peephole.

The sight that greeted her through the fish-eye lens was unexpected but immediately welcome. It was Rai – but she wasn't alone, and the stranger accompanying her sparked both curiosity and cautious hope in Kimberley's chest.

With hands that trembled slightly from leftover adrenaline, Kimberley opened the door, relief washing through her anew at the sight of her girlfriend's reassuring grin. The man beside Rai appeared to be in his late thirties, tall and broad-shouldered with the kind of solid presence that somehow managed to exude both unshakeable confidence and reassurance in equal measure. He wore a faded dark leather jacket over a plain t-shirt and comfortable-looking jeans, his thick, dark hair peppered with distinguished streaks of grey at the temples that spoke of experience rather than age. His eyes, sharp and observant beneath heavy brows that gave him a somewhat serious expression, softened noticeably as he smiled at Kimberley, immediately putting her more at ease.

"Kim, this is Dez," Rai said, her tone bright but tinged with barely contained urgency. Her curls were windswept, suggesting she'd been in a rush. "My cousin. Remember I told you about him? The one who had a dragon, back when we were kids. He's offered to help us."

Kimberley blinked, her thoughts racing, then quickly stepped back and gestured for them to come inside. She glanced down the hallway nervously before shutting the door behind them.

"Pleased to meet you, Kimberley," said Dez, his grip firm and steady as they shook hands. "Rai's told me everything. About the dragons. The lab. The plan... I've got a van ready to go, but there's a catch we need to discuss – it has to be tonight. My dad didn't ask too many questions when I borrowed it, but he'll need it back first thing in the morning."

"Tonight?" The word fell from Kimberley's lips like a stone into still water, her stomach instantly tightening into a hard knot.

"I know it's sudden," Rai said gently, her eyes full of understanding and quiet determination, "but this might be our only chance, Kim. We can do this. We have to."

Kimberley stood frozen for a moment, her mind running through all the possibilities – all the things that could go wrong, all the ways their plan could fall apart if they were to overlook even the smallest detail by being too hasty. But then she thought of the dragons, dozens of them, counting on them to make things right. Her resolve hardened, and she nodded decisively, squaring her shoulders. "Ok. Let's do it tonight."

They spent the next few hours in tense preparation, gathered around Kimberley's coffee table as they refined their plan with methodical precision. The dragon had taken up residence on Rai's lap, seemingly drawn by the intensity of their discussion like a moth to a flame. It watched them with those impossibly intelligent eyes as they worked out the details, its tail occasionally twitching in response to particularly demanding moments of conversation.

"We can't go before eleven," Kimberley insisted, spreading out the meticulously detailed notes she'd made about the lab's schedule across the coffee table like a general planning a military campaign. The papers rustled softly under her fingers as she pointed to specific times and schedules. "That's when everyone goes home for the night."

Rai nodded thoughtfully, her hand moving in absent patterns across the dragon's amethyst scales, drawing forth occasional pleased chirps. "The later we go, the less chance of anyone seeing us. The industrial estate is pretty much deserted at night."

"The van won't stand out in the shadows," Dez added, his presence acting as a steadying influence. "It's dark blue, practically invisible at night... I've parked it two blocks away. We can be at the lab in fifteen minutes once we get moving."

Each minute stretched as the clock crept towards their departure time. They tried to rest, knowing they'd need clear heads and steady hands, but it was impossible with all the anticipation thrumming through their veins like electricity. Kimberley paced the short length of the living area, the dragon watching from various perches, its eyes tracking her movement as it sensed her nervous energy. Rai alternated between reassuring Kimberley with gentle touches and words, and peppering Dez with questions about his childhood experience with his pet dragon. Dez answered each query with patience and warmth, his stories of his own dragon helping to pass the time until finally, mercifully, it was time to move.

The walk to the van felt endless, each shadow seemingly alive with potential witnesses, every distant sound making them freeze like startled deer. Kimberley held the dragon close beneath her jacket, feeling its warm weight against her ribs, its heart beating in perfect synchronisation with her own racing pulse. The night air was cool against her face, carrying the familiar sound of distant traffic that seemed surreal against the extraordinary nature of their mission.

"We'll need you to stay in the van," Rai told Dez as they approached the vehicle, her voice barely above a whisper but carrying the weight of absolute necessity. "And with him." She gestured to the dragon, who was peering out from beneath Kimberley's jacket like a curious child. "He shouldn't have to go back in there. The trauma..."

"I'll keep him safe," Dez promised, his expression as serious as a soldier accepting a sacred duty. "You just focus on getting the others out."

They drove in tense silence through the sleeping city, the van's headlights cutting through the darkness like blades as they made their way towards the industrial estate. Kimberley's magic hummed beneath her skin like a living thing, ready to be called upon, while beside her, Rai's hand found hers and squeezed gently, offering silent support.

Dez parked the van in the shadow of a tree-lined street near the lab, positioning it perfectly – close enough to load the dragons quickly, but hidden from the security cameras Kimberley would soon disable. He sat calmly behind the wheel, his steady presence a reminder that they weren't alone in this risky endeavour. Kimberley carefully lifted the dragon from beneath her jacket, placing it gently on Dez's lap. It settled immediately, but watched with concerned eyes as she prepared to leave.

Kimberley and Rai exchanged a final look, volumes of unspoken words passing between them before they slipped out of the van and into the night like shadows themselves. The lab loomed ahead, its harsh, sterile exterior illuminated by the cold glow of lights that made it look more like a prison than a research facility, which, ironically, was closer to the truth. Kimberley's heart raced like a frightened rabbit's, but she focused on the familiar hum of her magic, drawing it up like water from a deep well.

Just as she had during their last visit, Kimberley reached out with her magical senses, feeling for the web of security systems. Her fingers moved in subtle, practiced gestures as she carefully manipulated the threads of energy, deftly disabling cameras, convincing motion sensors to sleep, and finally, with a soft click that seemed to echo in the silence, unlocking the door.

The interior of the lab was even more oppressive at night, the emergency lights casting sickly shadows across the clinical surfaces that made everything look alien and unwelcoming. Their footsteps, despite their care, seemed impossibly loud on the polished floor; they moved with purpose, their earlier exploration having taught them the layout like a map etched in their memories.

The dragon room, when they reached it, was filled with the soft sounds of sleeping creatures, each breath and slight movement creating a gentle symphony of life in the sterile space. Cages lined the walls like metallic prison cells, each containing a dragon of different size and colour. Some stirred at their approach, lifting their heads with a mixture of fear and hope in their eyes that made Kimberley's heart ache.

"It's ok," she whispered, her magic already working on the first cage lock like a master key. "We're getting you out of here. All of you."

Rai moved alongside her with fluid grace, gathering each freed dragon in gentle arms, whispering soft words of comfort as she worked. They gestured to the more capable dragons, encouraging them to fly beside them, their wings creating soft whispers of movement in the still air. The dragons seemed to understand instantly, organising themselves with remarkable intelligence.

They worked in perfect synchronisation, Kimberley's magic making quick work of the locks while Rai ensured each dragon was safely carried or guided towards freedom.

The dragons, as if sensing the importance of silence, remained remarkably quiet, communicating through subtle movements and soft trills that seemed barely audible. Each one seemed to communicate with the others through some unspoken language, passing along clandestine messages that kept them calm and co-operative. They seemed to move with a firm understanding of the situation.

When the last cage door swung open with a soft click, Kimberley did a final sweep of the room, her heart pounding against her ribs. "That's all of them. Forty-two, just like in the records."

The journey from the lab to the van required multiple trips, each one more nerve-wracking than the last. Kimberley and Rai worked in tandem, guiding groups of dragons through the darkened corridors like shepherds leading their flock to safety. Each journey was a delicate balance of speed and caution, their hearts in their throats as they moved through the shadows.

"Everyone in?" Dez asked from the driver's seat, his voice low but clear.

Kimberley glanced at Rai, who gave a quick count of the dragons now packed into the van's cargo area, each one settled as comfortably as possible in the limited space. "All in. Go!"

The van pulled away smoothly, its tyres crunching softly against the gravel. Kimberley let out a shaky breath, the adrenaline coursing through her leaving her both exhilarated and exhausted, as if she'd run a marathon. Their amethyst dragon immediately moved to check on its freed companions, moving among them with gentle trills of comfort that seemed to ease the tension in the air.

As Dez navigated the route to the sanctuary, Kimberley worked tirelessly, using her magic to erase the identity tattoos from each dragon. The faint glow of her hands illuminated the van's interior like moonlight through water as she concentrated, the dragons watching her with a blend of curiosity and trust that touched her deeply. Their amethyst companion stayed close, occasionally nuzzling her side as if lending its support through the demanding task.

Finally, only one tattoo remained. Kimberley turned to the amethyst dragon, overwhelmed with emotion as she met its intelligent eyes. This was the dragon that had started it all, that had trusted her from the beginning, that had become so much more than just a rescued creature. Her hands trembled slightly as she reached out to touch its scales.

"Last one," she whispered, her voice thick with feeling. "After this, you're free. Really, properly free."

The dragon held perfectly still, watching her faithfully as her magic began to glow against its scales. The dark lines of the tattoo began to fade beneath her touch, disappearing like stars at dawn. As the last digit vanished, Kimberley felt tears prick at her eyes. The dragon was no longer property, no longer a lab specimen; it was simply itself, beautiful and wild and, most importantly, hers and Rai's – to love and protect for as long as they lived.

The amethyst dragon trilled softly, pressing its head against Kimberley's palm in a gesture of pure affection. In that moment, as her magic faded and the van carried them through the night, she knew with absolute certainty that the lab would never hurt these creatures again.

As the van's wheels continued to rumble over the tarmac, a different dragon, small and pink, caught Kimberley's attention. It seemed to gravitate towards their amethyst dragon as if pulled by an invisible force, the two of them exchanging soft trills and chirps that sounded like long-lost friends reuniting after years apart. Kimberley's heart warmed at the sight as she wondered about their shared history. Perhaps they had known each other back in the lab, sharing comfort through the bars of their cages, their friendship surviving despite the sterile cruelty of their captivity.

By the time they were nearing the sanctuary, Kimberley felt drained. She leaned heavily against Rai for support, grateful for her girlfriend's steady presence. Her magic felt like a guttering candle, barely able to maintain its flame after so much use.

The sanctuary gates loomed ahead, a sturdy structure flanked by tall hedges that rustled softly in the night breeze. Dez parked the van, and Kimberley and Rai stepped out into the cool night air, their nervousness visible in every movement as they approached the intercom.

Kimberley pressed the button with trembling fingers, the metal cold against her skin. For a long, uncomfortable moment, there was nothing but static, the sound seeming to stretch into eternity.

"Please let somebody be there," Rai whispered anxiously, looking up to the star-scattered sky as though addressing an invisible deity.

After what felt like an agonising wait, a woman's voice, warm but groggy with sleep, crackled through the static like a radio finding its frequency. "Hello?"

"Hi," Kimberley began, her voice shaky but urgent, every word feeling vital. "My name's Kimberley. We've rescued forty-two dragons from Romco Labs. They need a safe place. Please, we need your help."

There was a long pause, during which Kimberley's heart seemed to stop beating entirely, the world holding its breath. Then the gates began to creak open, the sound impossibly loud in the still of the night. A middle-aged woman emerged from a nearby building, pulling on a cardigan over her pyjamas, her movements quick and purposeful. Her expression was a mixture of shock and compassion as she approached along the gravel path.

"I'm Charlotte," she said, her voice kind but businesslike, carrying the authority of someone used to handling emergency situations. "Bring them in. All of them."

Kimberley and Rai moved to the back of the van, carefully lifting some of the dragons from their secure resting spots, their arms cradling the fragile creatures with gentle hands. Like living jewels in the night, the dragons' scales shimmered faintly, reflecting the moon's pale glow, each one unique and magnificent in its own way.

Charlotte moved ahead of them, guiding them through the sanctuary's vast grounds. With each step into this haven, Kimberley felt the weight of their journey beginning to lift from her shoulders. The rescued dragons seemed to sense it too – those strong enough to fly took tentatively to the air, perhaps a little bewildered by the sanctuary's nighttime beauty after a lifetime spent in sterile confinement. Tall trees whispered in the breeze, their leaves rustling softly, while flowers glowed faintly in the darkness, as though they too were in tune with the dragons. The distant sound of water trickling from a nearby fountain added to the serene atmosphere.

Kimberley's gaze lingered on the surroundings. The sanctuary wasn't just another facility – it was a refuge, a place where dragons could truly be themselves. The rescued dragons seemed to sense this too, their movements becoming slower and calmer as they glanced around their new environment with cautious wonder.

As they continued making trips between the van and the sanctuary, Charlotte led them towards the indoor area, where the warmth of a hearth greeted them, casting a soft amber light across the space. Kimberley let out a quiet breath of relief. Dragons of all colours and sizes were peacefully curled up on plush bedding, their forms nestled against soft, cushioned mats that looked more like luxury nests than simple resting places. There were no cold, barren cages here – only comfort and care.

The scent of fresh food lingered in the air, and Kimberley noticed bowls of nourishing meals scattered throughout the room. Each dragon seemed to eat at its own pace, and those already well-fed lay deep in restful sleep, their breathing slow and even. A large dragon, its emerald scales catching the firelight, rested with its wings draped across a bed of soft linens, while a smaller, more delicate dragon nestled comfortably beside it, its head tucked beneath the larger dragon's wing.

"It's beautiful here," Rai whispered in awe as they carried in another group of rescued dragons.

Kimberley nodded, full of gratitude. This wasn't just a place where dragons could survive; it was a place where they could thrive. Where they could feel safe, loved, and at peace.

Each journey back to the van felt lighter than the last, helped by the fact that every dragon they carried would soon be as content as those already sleeping peacefully in the sanctuary's embrace.

Kimberley felt exhaustion giving way to relief as the penultimate dragon crossed the threshold into the sanctuary.

The small pink dragon remained at the van's edge, its gaze fixed on the amethyst dragon as if unable to bear the thought of separation. It trilled questioningly. Kimberley looked at Rai, who met her eyes with a knowing smile that spoke of intense understanding.

"They seem to have a deep bond," Rai said softly, her voice full of comprehension and empathy. "It's too precious to break."

Kimberley nodded, her heart swelling with love for both the dragons and for Rai's immediate grasp of what needed to happen. "Then they'll stay together. With us."

Charlotte approached, her brow lifting in question as she noticed the two dragons still inside the van. Kimberley explained the situation, watching as an expression of approval spread across the sanctuary keeper's face.

"They'll be happy with you," Charlotte said. "Thank you for what you've done. For all of them."

The drive back to Kimberley's flat was quiet, but it was a different kind of quiet than before – peaceful rather than tense, filled with the soft sounds of two dragons crooning to each other in the back seat. It sounded just like a lullaby – gentle and comforting. Kimberley leaned against Rai, her body heavy with exhaustion but her mind more settled than it had been in days, floating on the knowledge of what they had accomplished. They had done it. They had actually done it, and the world felt full of possibility.

Chapter Nine

Morning sunlight streamed through the windows of Kimberley's flat, painting warm patches on the carpet. The amethyst dragon lay sprawled in one such spot, its scales creating tiny rainbow reflections on the wall as it basked. Beside it, the pink dragon was curled up like a cat, its rose-coloured scales shimmering with contentment as it dozed. Every now and then, one would shift slightly closer to the other, their bodies moving in unconscious synchronisation that spoke of deep trust and affection.

Kimberley watched them from her position on the couch, her legs tucked underneath her and a fresh cup of tea warming her hands. She couldn't help but marvel at how quickly the pink dragon had settled in. The past few days had been a revelation – watching the two dragons interact, seeing their distinct personalities emerge more fully.

"They're absolutely perfect together," Rai said softly, carrying her own steaming mug from the kitchen area. She settled onto the couch beside Kimberley, their shoulders touching comfortably. "Look at how the pink one always mirrors whatever position the amethyst one takes up."

As if to demonstrate this, the amethyst dragon stretched languorously in its patch of sunlight, and moments later, the pink dragon did the same, their movements flowing like a choreographed dance. Both dragons then turned their heads towards Kimberley and Rai, letting out harmonious trills of contentment that made both women laugh.

"It's like they're reading each other's minds," Kimberley agreed, leaning slightly into Rai's warmth. "Earlier this morning, I found them both perched on the bedroom windowsill, watching the birds together. The pink one was mimicking our little amethyst friend's head-tilting thing – you know, that thing it does when it's particularly interested in something?"

Rai smiled, reaching out to set her mug on the coffee table. "They're settling into such a lovely routine. It makes me so happy every time I come over and see them like this." She paused, her expression growing thoughtful. "Though I have to admit, it's getting harder to leave each time."

Kimberley's heart skipped a beat at these words, recognising in them an echo of her own feelings. The past few days had felt so natural – Rai coming over straight after work, spending every free moment together, creating their own little family unit in the cosy confines of the flat. When Rai wasn't there, the space felt somehow emptier, less complete.

"You know," Kimberley began, her voice soft but steady, "you don't have to leave." She turned slightly to face Rai better, their knees touching on the couch. "I mean... you could stay. Permanently."

The amethyst dragon lifted its head at this, as if sensing the importance of the moment. The pink dragon followed suit, both of them watching the conversation with obvious interest.

Rai's eyes widened slightly, a smile playing at the corners of her mouth. "Are you asking me to move in with you?"

"Yes," Kimberley said, feeling more certain with each passing second. "I know we've only been together eight months, but... it feels right, doesn't it? You're here most of the time anyway, and the dragons are so happy when we're all together. We could make it official – turn this into our home, all four of us."

The dragons trilled softly in what seemed like approval, making Kimberley and Rai laugh again, breaking any tension that might have built up in the moment.

"It does feel right," Rai agreed, reaching out to take Kimberley's hand. "It's like everything has fallen into place. We're already a family – we might as well make it official." She glanced around the flat with a considering eye. "Though we might need to invest in a few more cushions. Our scaled children seem to have claimed all the existing ones as their personal sunbathing spots."

Kimberley followed her gaze, noting how the dragons had indeed accumulated quite a collection of cushions and soft things around the flat, creating little nests in various sunny spots. "We can buy as many cushions as they want," she said, squeezing Rai's hand. "We can rearrange everything, make space for your things. Make it truly ours."

"I love that idea," Rai said, her smile widening. "Our home. Our family." She looked at the dragons, who were now watching them with unblinking attention. "What do you two think? Ready to make this arrangement permanent?"

The dragons responded with a melodious duet of happy trills, the amethyst one rising to its feet and padding over to them, the pink one following close behind. They settled closer to the couch, looking up at Rai and Kimberley with expressions that could only be described as joyful.

"I think that's a yes," Kimberley said with a chuckle, feeling as though her heart could burst with happiness.

The morning sunlight seemed to glow brighter, warming the scene like a blessing as they sat there together – Rai's hand in hers, their dragons at their feet, the future stretching out before them full of promise and possibility.

The amethyst dragon chirped questioningly, nudging Rai's ankle with its snout, while the pink one pressed against Kimberley's legs, their scales shimmering with contentment.

"Yes," Rai said with a chuckle, reaching down to scratch both dragons behind their ears. "We'll get started right away. Though I should warn you all – I have quite a lot of books. We might need another bookshelf or two."

"The more the better," Kimberley said. "We'll make space. We'll make everything work." She looked around her flat – their flat now – imagining how it would look with Rai's things mixed in with hers, their lives blending together just as naturally as the dragons' bond.

"Once we've got everything sorted and settled," Rai said softly, "we should visit the sanctuary and see how the other dragons are doing. It might be nice to make a donation while we're there. I'm sure they would appreciate it."

"Good idea." Kimberley smiled, leaning closer to Rai. "I'd love that. We can take these two with us – let them see their friends again." She watched as the dragons shifted closer together. "Though something tells me they're perfectly happy right where they are."

"Just like us," Rai murmured, pulling Kimberley closer.

The dragons trilled softly as Kimberley and Rai held each other in a tender embrace. In that moment, surrounded by love both human and dragon, Kimberley knew that everything was exactly as it was supposed to be.